CALMING THE STORM

Calming the Storm

Exercises leading to Contemplation

Carrin Dunne

Templegate Publishers
Springfield, Illinois

ISBN 0-87243-205-X

Contents

Introduction

The marvel of story is that we can enter into it, and so into another world. Through our bodies we are forced to live in the here and now, but through our souls we wander at large through all possible worlds. Story is our vehicle. The need to wander through space and time, to live out all the possibilities is, according to J.R.R. Tolkien, a primordial human desire, that is, a desire which has been with us from the beginning, from before the Fall, or a desire which issues from the very core of our being. It is not therefore a silly desire.[1] And a good story, a good steed, carries us into realms where Escape, Consolation and Recovery are available.[2]

Is Escape legitimate? Is Consolation true? Is Recovery possible? Escape from despair is always legitimate. Whatever allows the soul to draw a breath of fresh air, to find breathing-room, cannot be denied. It has no need to legitimate itself. It bears its efficacy upon its face. Tolkien identifies Consolation with the happy ending, the joyous "turn" of events. Not all stories, as they are told, have happy endings. Is it because the happy ending is an illusion, or is it because the storyteller does not always see far enough or deep enough?[3] Recovery has to

7

do with the recovery of sanity. It is the special province of the story we have chosen to study here.

Gospel stories are different from other stories in one crucial respect. Whereas other stories transport us in imagination from the confines of our present existence to another time, another place, another life, a Gospel story brings the Greater Time, the Greater Place, and the Greater Life into the confines of what may be a very ordinary, humdrum, nondescript or even a very painful existence, and explodes the prison walls. It reverses the direction, from a human gasp to a divine gust, blowing our way, refreshing the here and now, the "spot" where we have our human lives. It is more than an enlargement through Imagination; it is a transformation of the Actual.

Each Gospel story is in its own way an opening onto the total Mystery.[4] But each story is also placed by the Gospel writer in a context which gives it a peculiar slant, just as in the oral telling, even now when the written form of the Gospels has given them a certain fixity, a story shapes itself to fit the needs and situation of a particular audience. There are also subtle techniques employed in both oral and written forms which affect our understanding in vital ways. One of these techniques is Mark's habit of beginning a story, then telling another story as a kind of aside or something which happened along the way, and finally returning to and completing the first story.[5] What we are given is a story within a story, where one functions as the "inside story" and the other functions as the frame story.

How does an inside story function? We expect it to provide more intimate revelations which are somehow key to a proper understanding of the frame story. If so, the story of the calming

8

of the storm should provide a key to understanding what is happening in the story of the healing of the demoniac. Some things to notice right away are, first of all, the location of the two stories. The story of the healing of the demoniac begins on one shore and ends on the other, while the story of the calming of the storm takes place at sea. Symbolically, what occurs on land takes place at a more conscious level than what occurs at sea. Sea stories often refer to the deeper, more secret processes occurring at unconscious levels of our being, as articulated poetically by the Psalmist: "Thy way is in the sea, and thy path in the great waters, and thy footsteps are not known" (Ps. 77).

A second point to notice is that while only the closest disciples are present at the calming of the storm, the healing of the demoniac is attended by the disciples, the demoniac himself along with the legion of demons who have taken possession of him, a herd of pigs, the pigherders, and finally the populace of city and countryside who have come out to see. One is a very private scene, while the other concerns a large public. This difference casts light on a strange saying which in Mark's account precedes the telling of the two related stories. "Unto you it is given to know the mystery of the kingdom of God: but unto them that are without, all things are done in parables" (4:11). The closest disciples are granted a privileged witnessing, which is not to say that their understanding of what they experience is superior. As we shall see, the only character in our story who truly understands is the healed sufferer.

A third point to notice is the simplicity of the key story by comparison with the frame story, which is not to say that it is easier to grasp. Actually, the key story is much more challenging in that it holds within itself the mystical secret, one which proves to be a stumbling-block and a scandal for the closest disciples, one which will also put each of us to the test. The frame story is more complex. There are many more tangles to sort out. It keeps our minds busy with a kind of detective work, figuring out who's who and what's what, whereas the key story just puts it to us, calling upon us not to figure out, but simply to be or to become. The key story is, of course, an image of the essence, while the frame story is an image of the outcomes.[6]

If a Gospel story is an opening onto the total Mystery, it deserves to be heard and read in such a way that we can by so doing enter into the Mystery. It is done most perfectly within the context of the liturgy of the Eucharist. But there can also be for the individual or for small groups a kind of remote preparation or prolongation of the Eucharist through spiritual exercises such as are proposed here. These exercises are field work, preparing the soil by weeding, turning, aerating and fertilizing, awaiting the unseen rain which alone produces the miracle.[7] I call them "exercises leading to contemplation." There is a preference in the Christian tradition for the word 'prayer' over the word 'meditation,' and in the Catholic tradition for the word 'contemplation,' as indicative of the highest form of prayer. In both cases the motivation is the same. It is the deep-seated conviction that God is the doer, and that our only helpful doing is undoing, clearing the ground, preparing the soil, waiting and watching.[8]

Exercises leading to contemplation could be translated "doings leading to undoing." What kind of undoing? The kind that simplifies life, leaving it happy and free. The kind that stills the mind so that it may know God. The kind that frees the heart to repose on the mother's breast like a weaned child. The

10

kind that supples the body like a green tree planted by the rivers of water. It is rendered specific by the theme of the story, in this case the calming of a storm, of violence without and violence within, and its outcome, a recovery of sanity. We are left contemplating the LORD and/or contemplating his parable, the healed man freed of his demons, and asking, "WHO is this, that even the wind and the sea obey him?" WHO is the ultimate Christian koan, an endless discovery.

Why did I choose this particular Gospel story? I don't know. The thought of it kept coming back and back, insistently. I think it chose itself.

Here are a few practical suggestions for those who choose to use the exercises. Keep a kind of looseleaf journal of your experiences with the exercises, your reflections afterwards, what you want to remember from others' experience with the same (in the event that there is some group sharing), one you can add to from time to time, one capacious enough to include your art work.

The exercises proposed were devised to accord with the character of the narrative point under consideration. I am increasingly convinced that the various methods of meditation and prayer proposed by different religious traditions presuppose certain fundamental beliefs with regard to God, self, and world. In other words, the method is shaped by the underlying story, **logos** is shaped by **mythos**. In the present work, where the story is taken as a representation of the total Mystery under one of its aspects, the underlying connection between story and method is made explicit. The purpose of the exercises is to enter the story as fully as possible, and to allow yourself to be made anew by the transforming power of the sacred story.

The exercises are also meant to develop the soul in a variety of ways. **Reflections** call upon and develop the powers of the conscious mind, allowing you to come to know your own mind, what you really believe and value, where you take your stand. **Recollections** delve into the well of memory and by re-membering experiences scattered over time, enable you to achieve simultaneity, the substance of presence at any given moment. The visions are generated through expressive arts which reach deep down into the body, to that hidden and humble place where the known unknown dwells, where feeling and imagination are kindled. They bring to consciousness treasures heretofore hidden in the unconscious or, to use an older language they bring **heart to mind.** Then there are meditative exercises, some body-centered, some mantric, which bring mind **down into heart**, nearing the ineffable Presence which deigns to reside there. Those which move from heart to mind are towards the Word; those which move from mind to heart are towards the Silence. All are chosen with a view to contemplation, to becoming a temple of the LORD, a sanctuary, a refuge for all in need, a center, a place of communion between heaven and earth.

Not all of the exercises will be suitable for the needs of each person. For those who have already reached a deep level of union, such aids are dispensable altogether. If you should find yourself shying away from a certain exercise, however, be sure to ask yourself why. If it is just an unnecessary distraction, then skip it with a free heart. If it is because it is too demanding, then try to be honest with yourself about that. If it is because such activities seem childish and embarrassing, remember that in the learning of prayer one cannot become too childlike.

1. Reynolds Price writes, "A need to tell and hear stories is essential to the species Homo sapiens — second in necessity apparently after nourishment and before love and shelter. Millions survive without love or home, almost none in silence..." (*A Palpable God, New York, 1978, p. 3*).

2. These ideas are developed in Tolkien's essay, "On Fairy-Stories," in *Tree and Leaf* (Boston, 1965).

3. Reynolds Price continues, "The need is not for the total consolation of narcotic fantasy — our own will performed in airless triumph — but for credible news that our lives proceed in order toward a pattern which, if tragic here and now, is ultimately pleasing in the mind of a god who sees a totality and at last enacts His will. We crave nothing less than a perfect story..." (Ibid., p. 14).

4. "...among the revelations of Bible narrative is its vast demonstration that the most complex material imaginable may be contained and offered in lucid forms" (Reynolds Price, op. cit., p. 17.).

5. My attention was drawn to this Markan technique by Werner Kelber's insightful *Mark's Story of Jesus* (*Philadelphia, 1979*), p. 32.

6. Other examples of what is sometimes called the "sandwich" technique in Mark are the story of the healing of Jairus' daughter (Mk. 5:21-43), where the healing of the woman with the issue of blood is the inside story (5:25-34) or meat of the sandwich, and the story of the feeding of the five thousand (Mk. 6:30-52 and Jn. 6:1-59), where the story of Jesus walking on water (Mk. 6:45-51 and Jn. 6:16-21) is key.

The frame story/key story relationship might be compared to that of the spoken and unspoken Tao in the first poem of Lao Tzu's *Tao Te Ching*. While the inside story is told in words, just like the frame story, it also contains an unspoken core, a mystical secret. Lao Tzu offers a clue to how the secret is perceived.

Ever desireless, one can see the mystery. (the essence)
Ever desiring, one can see the manifestations. (the outcomes)
These two spring from the same source but differ in name;
this appears as darkness.
Darkness within darkness.
The gate to all mystery.
(trans. Gia-Fu Feng and Jane English...my additions in parentheses)

7. This lovely image, unseen rain, is taken from the title given to a translation of the quatrains of the Muslim mystic, Rumi, by John Moyne and Coleman Barks (Putney, VT, 1986).

8. A connection could be made to the Taoist notion of *wu-wei*, which means literally "non-doing," but which in practice means not only "not interfering," "not diverting" from the true Way, but includes helpful activities, such as unblocking, clearing, simplifying, etc., whatever allows a freer flowing of the Tao.

The Story
According to Mark

(The Key Story is in indented italics within the Frame Story)

That same day, when evening was come, he said to them, Let us pass over unto the other side.

And there arose a great windstorm, and the waves beat into the boat, so that it was now full. And he was in the back of the boat, asleep on a cushion: and they awoke him, saying, Master, do you not care that we perish? And he arose, and rebuked the wind, and said unto the sea, **Peace, be still.** *And the wind ceased, and there was a great calm. And he said to them,* **Why are you so fearful? How is it that you have no faith?** *And they feared a great fear, and said to one another, Who is this, that even the wind and the sea obey him?*

And they came over unto the other side of the sea, into the country of the Gadarenes. And when he stepped out of the boat, immediately there met him out of the tombs a man with an unclean spirit, who made his dwelling among the tombs; and no man could bind him, no, not with chains: because he had been often bound with fetters and chains, and he had broken the chains and smashed the fetters in pieces: neither could anyone tame him. And always, night and day, he was in the mountains, and in the tombs, crying, and cutting himself with stones. But when he saw Jesus afar off, he ran and fell at his feet, and cried out with a loud voice, saying, What have I to do with you, Jesus, Son of the Most High God? I adjure you by God, torment me not. For he was saying to him, **Unclean spirit, come out of the man.** And he asked him, **What is your name?** And he answered, my name is legion: for we are many. And he entreated him not to send them away out of the country. Now a great herd of pigs were feeding there near the mountain. And all the demons begged him, saying, Send us into the swine, let us enter into them. And forthwith Jesus gave them leave. And coming out, the unclean spirits entered into the pigs: and the herd rushed down the cliff and into the sea (they were about two thousand) and were drowned. And those who fed the pigs fled, and spread the news to city and countryside. And those who heard came out to see what had happened.

And they came to Jesus, and stared at the demoniac, the one possessed by the legion, sitting, and clothed, and in his right mind: and they were afraid. And the pigherders related to them what had happened to the demoniac and to the pigs.

And they started begging Jesus to leave their territory. Once he had gotten back into the boat, the former demoniac prayed to stay with him. But Jesus did not allow it, saying to him, **Go home to your own people, and tell**

them the great things the LORD has done for you, and how he has had compassion on you. And the man departed, and spread the news through the Ten Cities of the great things Jesus had done for him. And all marvelled. (Mark 4:35-5:20).

See also Matthew 8:18, 23-34 and Luke 8: 22-39.

1
Let Us Pass Over

Many complain that the words of the wise are always merely parables and of no use in daily life, which is the only life we have. When the sage says: "Go over," he does not mean that we should cross to some actual place, which we could do anyhow if the labor were worth it; he means some fabulous yonder, something unknown to us, something too that he cannot designate more precisely, and therefore cannot help us here in the very least.
(trans. Will and Edwin Muir)

In his small masterpiece, "On Parables," Franz Kafka sums up the teaching of the wise in two words, "Go over." The words are so simple, so everyday. Such an instruction should be easy to follow, shouldn't it? Why then do we have such difficulty? Is it that we don't know WHERE to go? Or we do not know HOW? Or is the prospect of such a transition too frightening to attempt?

Then there is the question WHY? Why make such a displacement? (How big a displacement is it? Is it a quantum leap?). In Kafka's words, "If you only followed the parables you yourselves would become parables and with that be rid of all your daily cares." To be rid of the burden of daily cares is inviting indeed. One who promises that his burden is light (Mt. 11:30) points the way to carefreeness in the story within the story (the sea crossing). The demoniac both in his suffering condition and especially as healed exemplifies someone who has become a parable.

A sage may advise a disciple, "Go over," but it is something the disciple must accomplish alone. Only the LORD can support the disciple from within.

Experience the difference between GO OVER and LET US PASS OVER to the other side.

2
The Other Side

According to Pirke Aboth (*Sayings of the Fathers*), the Men of the Great Synagogue bequeathed three things to the later rabbis: to be deliberate in judging, to raise up many disciples, and to make a hedge or protective encirclement for the Torah. By inviting his disciples to pass over to the other side, Jesus is calling them beyond the hedge of Torah. On the other side of the sea of Galilee is pagan territory, the land of the ten cities or Decapolis. The 'other side' (*sitra ahra* in Aramaic) is a dangerous place, the abode of Satan, of forces which feed on filth and which try to overpower and seduce. The Shekinah herself (she is the Divine Presence on earth in its feminine and earthy mode such as the Burning Bush or the Cloud on Sinai) is threatened by it, except on the Sabbath when she is united in the secret of One (that is, joined with the masculine or heavenly mode of that same Presence).

But the other side or farther shore is also a symbol of the 'beyond,' which we call heaven. When Jesus invites his disciples to pass over with him to the other side, it could very well be construed to mean entering the kingdom of heaven, particularly in the light of the cosmic event which occurs in the course

21

of the crossing and of its existential counterpart, the calming
of the demoniac on the other side.

It is a curious fact that words often bear opposite meanings.
So it is with the 'other side.' It is at once a leading into
temptation and the entryway to heaven.

Reflection: But where and how do the opposites coincide?

The *Zohar* comments:

Come and see the secret of the word:
If Abram had not gone down into Egypt
and been refined there first,
he could not have partaken of the Blessed Holy One.
Similarly with his children,
when the Blessed Holy One wanted to make them unique,
a perfect people,
and to draw them near to Him:
If they had not gone down to Egypt
and been refined there first,
they would not have become His special ones.

So too the Holy Land:
If she had not been given first to Canaan to control,
she would not have become the portion, the share
of the Blessed Holy One.

It is all one mystery.

[*ZOHAR: The Book of Enlightenment*, tr. Daniel Chanan Matt. New York: Paulist Press, 1983, 1983, p. 64. A mystical commentary on the Pentateuch which forms the centerpiece of Spanish-Jewish Kabbalah, composed by Moses de Leon, in the late thirteenth century.]

3
Vision I
Let Us Pass Over Unto The Other Side

Stand and sweep your arm in front of your face to describe a horizon line. Move from left to right using your right hand and arm, then from right to left using the left hand and arm. Swivel from the hips with the movement. Let your whole body move from the soles of your feet upward. Continue the movement until you are fully into it, until your whole being is describing the distant horizon.

Now, on a sheet of paper, preferably a good piece of drawing paper, draw a light line across it near the top, describing the farther shore. Not a perfectly straight line as though drawn with a ruler, but a living line. The sheet is now divided into two parts: the sea to be crossed below, the other side to be reached above. We begin by projecting a goal to be reached, here called "the other side." We begin by projecting our hopes and fears. What awaits us on the other side?

Our task is not to draw a picture. We are not trying to make a reasonably correct representation of what the other side of the sea of Galilee may have looked like in the light of evening to Jesus and his disciples from where they stood. Nor are we concerned with making art. Such a concern would be not only severely inhibiting, forbidding to those without artistic talent, but would lead us off track. Our concern is **contemplation**, an envisioning of what lies hidden beneath the surface of things and events. Ours is not to be a skillful rendering of what the outer eye observes, but an artless expression of an inner life. Once that expression has found its way from the heart through the hand to the paper, then it can be contemplated. We are not recording a vision (an already formed image viewed by the inner eye), but **generating a vision**. We shall not know what it is that we see until the picture is finished. The picture slowly emerges from the unconscious, arising in the heart as inchoate feeling, moving through arm and hand onto paper to produce a "something," a kind of mystery.

If you haven't a clue how to begin, so much the better. The more "innocent" your picture is in the making, the richer it will be for purposes of contemplation. If your imagination is not immediately triggered by "the other side" as the place of your hopes and fears, take a few moments to get in touch with your fears. Try finding a drum beat which expresses how your fears feel to you. You don't need to use a drum; you can just beat your hands against a table surface, or bang on pots and pans. What color(s) do you associate with your fears? Then shift from fears to hopes. Find a rhythm to express your hopes and beat it out to really feel it. Then find the color(s) of your hopes. Now you are ready to put the hopes and fears on paper as a movement of color.

Use whatever color medium (crayons, pastels, watercolors, etc.) appeals to you. Don't begin with your brain. Let your hand decide what movements it wants to make with the colors to express hope and fear. Remember that color is feeling. What you put down may be an abstract swirl of color; it may be ugly. What matters is whether it feels "right," whether it expresses your hopes and fears accurately. Let one movement lead to another. Be willing to just stare at the unfinished work for long moments until you are moved spontaneously to continue.

Once you feel you have done enough to "the other side," shift your focus to the expanse which must be crossed in order to reach it. "It furthers one to cross the greater water." So says the *I Ching*, the ancient Chinese oracle book. Jesus says, "Let us pass over...," promising to be with us for the long haul, more present to us than we are to ourselves.

Does the sea of Galilee qualify as a "great water"? It is not even a great lake, much less a sea. But its greatness has nothing to do with size and everything to do with what happened there, with the events it witnessed, and with what it has come to symbolize, as in our story.

Again our task is not to render the look of the sea at twilight, but to express the multitude of our feelings in the crossing of it. You might consider **phases of your life** as stretches of the sea to be crossed, choosing colors which have the feel of those phases. At some point the process may begin to move forcefully on its own. If so, let it take the reins and go where it chooses. Understanding comes afterwards.

CONTEMPLATION

Sitting quietly facing the image, do not try to analyze it. If it speaks to you, listen. If it moves you, be with the emotion. If it bothers you, stay with the bother. If you have an urge to make a small change in the picture, make it. If you want to tear it up, be merciful instead and let it live. Be with it and let it be with you.

A note on Generating a Vision:

The great Swiss psychologist, C.G. Jung, relates in his autobiography (*Memories, Dreams, Reflections*) that the emergence from unconsciousness to consciousness follows a certain progression: (1) *childplay* (he allowed himself at age thirty-seven to follow an urge to gather stones by the lake shore and to build cottages, a castle, a whole village, even a church, remarking: "This moment was a turning-point in my fate, but I gave in only after endless resistances and with a sense of resignation. For it was a painfully humiliating experience to realize that there was nothing to be done [in order to re-establish contact with the creative impulse] except play childish games" (p. 174)). Expressive arts in the way we are using them might be looked upon as forms of childplay. Play unleashes (2) *emotions*. "I was frequently so wrought up that I had to do certain yoga exercises in order to hold my emotions in check... To the extent that I managed to translate the emotions into (3) *images* — that is to say, to find the images that were concealed in the emotions — I was inwardly calmed and reassured. Had I left those images hidden in the emotions, I might have been torn to pieces by them" (p. 177). He goes on: "I took great care to try to understand every single image...and, above all, to realize them in actual life. That is what we usually neglect to do. We allow the images to rise up, and maybe we wonder about them, but that is all. We do not take the trouble to understand them, let alone draw ethical conclusions from them. This stopping-short conjures up the negative effects of the unconscious" [e.g. psychic inflation, exaggeration, unreality, split between outer and inner life] (p. 192). "It is equally a grave mistake to think that it is enough to gain some understanding of the images and that knowledge can here make a halt. (4) *Insight* into them must be converted into an (5) *ethical obligation*" (p. 193).

It might be objected that in the "Contemplation" I have stopped short at the third level, staying with the image without analyzing it. What I mean to do is to slow down and deepen the process. If you have completed the exercise, what you have before you is an image of your whole life in its various phases up to the present moment, heading towards the unknown, the place of hopes and fears. It is a vast image, even a revelation. It is not something to be passed over quickly, then on to the next subject. There is the matter of staying with the vision, of **being with it**, of allowing it to be with you. I believe that understanding comes of its own accord in due time, and that the quality of the understanding, as well as of the moral transformation which follows upon it, will depend directly upon the degree of staying power, of being with which is brought to bear on the initial gift of vision. Consider Julian of Norwich who received her Showings on a single day, 13 May 1373, at the age of thirty, and remained with them for the rest of her life, slowly distilling a most wonderful theology. Meanwhile, what Jung calls "conjuring up the negative effects of the unconscious" can be forestalled by the humble realization that we do not fully understand what has been given to us, or why.

It might also be objected that "generating" a vision is not to be compared to a vision which comes unsought as a pure gift from God. I would answer that usually there has been significant, if indirect, groundwork preparatory to the most surprising of visions, and that even an induced vision (acquired contemplation as opposed to infused) encompasses a large amount of spontaneity. The telling difference between one vision and another is not the manner of the vision, but the purity and humility of the heart/mind which receives it.

C.G. Jung. *Memories, Dreams, Reflections (New York, 1961).*

4
THE BOAT'S ORDEAL

Sudden storms are frequent over the sea of Galilee, when winds off the Mediterranean meet the hot desert winds of Syria. Storms are frequent in human life as well, also caused by conflicting winds, the conflicts of vying spirits.

If you were to place yourself in the situation, in contemplation, you might begin by imagining yourself as the boat. Caught by the storm in the middle of the lake, too far from either shore, battered and in danger of breaking apart, filling up with water, you have within you a multitude of discordant and panicky voices (the disciples), all struggling and failing to gain control over you. There is also within you a great calm Presence, but it is dormant.

Insofar as you are your body, you are the boat. You bear a precious cargo. You have a great task, to bear that cargo from here to there, from this shore to the farther shore, from the land of promise to the other side. You are a sturdy craft but vulnerable to the forces of nature. You are not in control. All you can do is what you were built to do, until the moment arrives when you succumb to the interplay of more powerful forces.

31

How is the LORD present to the boat? According to Mark's testimony, Jesus was in the back of the boat, asleep on a pillow. So he is IN the boat, present through **indwelling**, his own body sharing the fate of the boat. He is also at a deep (not a surface) level of awareness WITH the boat, in the words of the Canticle, "I sleep, but my heart waketh" (Ct. 5:2).

Cf. Shelley Wachsmann. *"The Galilee Boat." Bibl. Arch. R.,* Sept./Oct. 1988, vol. XIV, #5, pp. 18-33 for an idea of what the boat may have looked like.

INDWELLING Meditation.

Close your eyes and let your mind move freely through your body, pausing at points of tension, discomfort or pain until called away by some other spot in the body which seeks attention. Don't visualize the spot, just feel it, **be with it** as the LORD is with the boat. Like the LORD asleep in the boat, do no try to change anything. Don't try to relieve the tension or ease the discomfort. Don't try to hold it in place either. Just **be with** the feeling in a compassionate, non-judgmental sort of way.

Sometimes your body will make subtle readjustments on its own. One benefit of this form of meditation, particularly if it is practiced with some frequency, is a reintegration of mind and body. Another benefit is a diminishing of fear of pain. A third benefit is that the mind begins to learn what the body already knows. And so on...

Learn from the practice of Indwelling the value of simple presence.

5
Vision II
CAUGHT BY THE STORM.

Once again it is not a matter of drawing a boat caught in a storm, but of expressing through movement and color the experience of being **overwhelmed**. Yet not that alone. At the heart of the storm is a Presence of unfathomable peace. The LORD asleep within the boat is like the Eye of the storm. Our own experience (as boat battered by the storm but bearing the indwelling Presence) is one of paradox, **perishing** and at the same time **enjoying** the peace that passes understanding.

You might want to begin in movement, a kind of free-form dancing the experience of being battered by a storm, of hovering at the edge of death. Movement allows the body a chance to speak, the body itself being a repository of immense knowledge which has not yet been brought to mind. The engagement of the whole body in the movement is also the most powerful way of entering fully into an experience, here the experience of being overwhelmed. It taps deep memories of all the overwhelming experiences you have endured in the past, bringing them together within the sacred confines of the Gospel story.

In the very throes of your Dance of Death you suddenly realize that something else is coming to bear on your dire situation. There is something/someone within you which knows no fear, which is utterly secure, which quietly radiates strength, light, and an unspeakable peace. Your dance changes of itself. How does it change?

While resting from the exertion, let your imagination shift from movement to color in order both to preserve the experience and to explore it in another way. What colors would you choose for your Death dance? What colors for the arrival of Peace?

Try holding on to both sides of the experience as you choose your colors and let your hand begin to move. Or you may want to make the picture with both hands, one expressing the violence of the storm, the other making peace.

Do not be concerned if the end product is not pretty or if it makes no sense to anyone but you (and the LORD). What another person would see in your vision would reflect his/her own relationship to Life and death, not yours.

CONTEMPLATION

Which hand made war, and which made peace? Where in the vision is your fear, your pain, your grief? Where is your joy and your peace? How do the opposites relate to one another? How does it feel to hold the opposites together? Where are the surprises?

6
THEY AWOKE HIM

The Psalms are full of attempts to awaken the LORD. "Awake, why sleepest thou, O LORD? arise, cast us not off for ever. Wherefore hidest thou thy face, forgetting our affliction and oppression?" (Ps. 44: 23-24). Psalm 44 even contains a reproach similar to the one voiced by the disciples in Mark's account.

The amazing thing from our point of view is that the storm, terrible and life-threatening as it was, failed to awaken him. He must have been unusually exhausted to sleep through it. Or else he wasn't really troubled by it. Knowing his own power, he remained tranquil in a situation which panicked the disciples.

He does respond immediately when the disciples call out to him. It could be argued that the storm and the plight of the boat made no direct appeal to him, being but the interplay of blind forces, that only the human being can turn to the LORD and address him by name. But the storyline indicates clearly that the disciples did the wrong thing, that their appeal was not a cry of faith but a failure of faith.

Reflection: Where did they go wrong?

The Canticle may provide a clue. There is a refrain thrice repeated (2:7; 3:5; 8:4) which works through the song like a leitmotif.

I adjure you, O daughters of Jerusalem,
By the gazelles, and the hinds of the field:
Do not wake or rouse
Love until it please!

The daughters of Jerusalem function somewhat like a Greek chorus in the song. Privy to the secrets of the two lovers, they are a higher form of consciousness, which, as "daughters" or "maidens," is in the feminine mode, open, flexible and receptive, perhaps even virginal, certainly fertile and capable of bearing fruit. They are charged in the name of the gazelles and the deer, swift, easily startled creatures of steppe and forest — that is, of both the open and hidden planes of reality. It seems to be an admonition to go softly so as not to disturb delicate stirrings, subtle processes which, if they are to come to fruition, require on our part gentleness, self-restraint and trust. "And he said, So is the kingdom of God, as if a man should cast seed into the ground; and should sleep, and rise night and day, and the seed should spring and grow up, he knoweth not how" (Mk. 4:26-27).

Consider once again the secret: **"I sleep, but my heart waketh."** The 'I' must be put to sleep for the 'heart' to awaken. Are the disciples pulling Jesus back to the level of 'I,' the only level of reality they understand?

7
Vision III
I SLEEP, BUT MY HEART
WAKETH

Have you ever really forgotten yourself, even for a moment? Have you ever experienced your heart breaking open or opening softly, like a flower? Did these moments of self-forgetting and opening coincide?

We may indeed remember occasions when something of the sort took place, but it is unlikely that the transition itself is remembered consciously. How could we remember consciously where consciousness leaves off? Such moments are known only in retrospect. "I was here, then I was there. But how did I get from here to there?"

How then can we re-enter such an experience in order to dwell in it? We can let the body take the lead. Our bodies know how to do all sorts of things of which we are unaware consciously. The body also remembers everything, even those things which have never entered consciousness.

Ask your body to be your wise guide. You might proceed by asking your body leading questions: "How do 'I' fall asleep?" "Where is my heart?" "How does my heart awaken?"

"To what does my heart awaken?" Let your body express itself as it chooses...through posture, gesture, movement, making sounds, etc. What comes may be very subtle, still far below the threshold where words begin.

Since what you are attempting to render is a mystery (beyond the 'I' and its consciousness), it is best to proceed as it were blindly. Not necessarily with your eyes closed (though that might be one way to do it), but without preconceptions. At some point invite your hands to move color beyond mind. Leave room for additional surprises.

What may be hoped for in the making of a picture is to enter a mystery. What may be hoped for in the finished picture is that through contemplation something of the mystery may be revealed.

CONTEMPLATION

In your mind picture the LORD sleeping through the storm. Put that mental picture together with the one your hands have made. Does the one illuminate the other?

"He gives to his beloved while they sleep (Ps. 127)." Be willing to look at your finished picture for long moments. Let it be your teacher. Come back to it again and again.

A Note on Sleeping and Waking:

The Note on Generating a Vision attempts to explicate in a general way what the Introduction calls "bringing heart to mind." Here, we are still moving in that same direction, which is the purpose of all the Visions, but the subject-matter of Vision III is its opposite, "bringing mind down into heart." We find ourselves in the strange situation of trying to explain "bringing mind down into heart" by "bringing heart to mind." Bringing mind down into heart is only understood directly through the meditative exercises which serve as vehicles to take us in that direction, such as the Indwelling meditation which we have already experienced, the Letting Go meditation just ahead, and mantric meditations yet to come. Trying to put into words what happens when mind is brought down into and united with heart (heart meaning not just the seat of emotions, but what Meister Eckhart called the "core" of the soul, there where we encounter the Indwelling Presence) tends to stand words on their heads. Not only is our effort something of a contradiction in terms (it is why mystics insist that the experience of union cannot be told), it involves us in paradox. Sleeping is really waking (in the True sense), while waking (in the ordinary sense) is sleeping.

That said, I believe the clearest, simplest and most profound explication of **"I sleep, but my heart waketh"** may be found in the *Mandukya Upanishad,* which is one of the principal texts of Hindu religious thought, and which is held by Hindu believers to be sufficient of itself to lead to *moksha* or liberation. The *Mandukya* presents four levels of "consciousness" (that is, consciousness standing on its head, where what we ordinarily call consciousness is seen as the lowest level, and what modern psychology has taught us to call the "unconscious" encloses the higher levels), symbolically associated with the greatest of mantras, AUM.

The first or lowest level of "consciousness" is the waking state, dominated by the 'I' at its center, where what is known is the external physical world. It is associated with the sound A.

The second level is the dream state, associated with the sound U, which presents us with the internal world, that is, the predispositions whereby we understand external phenomena. These predispositions take the form of images generated by what Freud called the "wish." It is reality at a subtler and more fluid state than what we know externally as gross material objects. At this level the 'I' is subtle and fluid as well. Sometimes the 'I' plays a role in dreams, sometimes it is a silent and invisible observer. It might even be said that every element of the dreamscape and every player in it is in some respect an aspect of 'I.'

The third level is deep sleep, where images and desires and the 'I' itself disappear. The *Mandukya* calls this state *prajna*. It is union with God where the mind sinks into its core, where mind and heart become one. It can be called "consciousness" because thought waves emerge from this core. It is an experience in so much as it is the source of the bliss and peace which suffuses the saints (though it may be a bliss and peace of which they are sometimes consciously unaware). It is associated with the sound M (cf. humming as a meditative mode).

But then there is a fourth level, simply called "the fourth." It is referred to as transcendent consciousness. Perhaps it could also be called consciousness of transcendence. The best clue to what it is is to be found, I believe, in the associated sound symbols. There is no separate fourth sound associated with the fourth level. Rather it is the first three sounds taken together

A-U-M as one complete mantra. It suggests to me that the fourth level really is the first three levels all together. It is precisely the situation we find ourselves in in meditation, where we remain awake and conscious (level A), but through a vehicle (level U) send the mind like an arrow towards its heart-core (level M). To this the great Hindu teacher, Shankara, adds: "The knowledge of the fourth is attained by merging the (previous) three in the order of the previous one in the succeeding one."* It might be represented graphically as 彌. In meditation what really counts is the moment of union M, which cannot be measured. A flow of imagery and thought may be going on simultaneously 彌 without hindering union, so long as the intention remains pure. And there is great advantage in the meditative state over ordinary waking, dreaming and deep sleep in that the concurrence of wakefulness 彌 allows for remembering, that is, for integrating conscious and unconscious.

*Quoted in S. Radhakrishnan, *The Principal Upanishads* (London: 1969), p. 695.

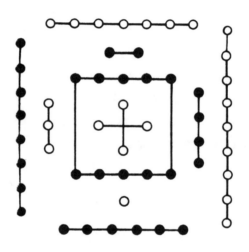

8
DO YOU NOT CARE?

Perhaps it is too simplistic to say that prayer is the expression of faith. In Matthew's "LORD, save us: we perish" and Luke's "Master, Master, we perish," what looks and sounds like prayer is, according to Jesus' response, an expression of unfaith. All the more so in Mark, where the outcry takes the form of an accusation: "Master, do you not care that we perish?", and is answered by the harshest reproach: "How is it that you have no faith?"

In Mark's story the disciples are not only unable to intuit the value of Jesus' sleeping Presence to them, to the boat, to the storm; they misread it from the perspective of their own limitations. We can imagine them thinking, "If I were to sleep like that, straight through a crisis, leaving the others to bear the brunt of it and carry on the struggle alone, it could only mean that I didn't care what happened to them and couldn't be bothered to help out."

The "do you not care?" is perilously close to "you do not care." It is but a hair's breadth away from rupturing the relationship.

Reflection: How can we learn not to prejudge (cf. prejudice) what we fail to understand?

Sometimes we must learn the hard way by making drastic mistakes, causing grief to others and to ourselves. But we can also practice letting go of thoughts and desires momentarily, a practice which puts a tiny distance between our heart and our illusions/delusions, and which can be in itself an unspoken prayer for liberation. The disciples were caught up in the terror of the moment. They reacted blindly, and not from the best place in themselves. With practice habits are formed which in the long run can become second nature. In the tiny gap between heart and its illusions there is room for the Holy Spirit to breathe.

LETTING GO Meditation

It is impossible to have no thoughts/desires except in the state of deep sleep. What can be learned is how to drop momentarily a particular train of thought as you become aware of it. Give your mind a very simple focus. For instance, follow your breathing mindfully. When you breathe, notice how the air feels cool entering your nostrils and warm coming out. Notice how you open up on the inhalation and tighten on the exhalation. Just breathe naturally, but feel the breath going in and out. Following the breath occupies the mind without preoccupying it. But soon you will notice that your mind has drifted back to its preoccupations. When you catch yourself, acknowledge the thought and the desire the way you might nod and greet a couple of passersby, then go on about your business of following the breath. Sometimes the random thought may be a creative idea, an inspiration or a solution to a problem. You will be sorely tempted to pursue it. Acknowledge it, give thanks for it, and promise to come back to it later. Then let it move on past you as you return to following the breath.

There are many benefits to the practice of following the breath, but the only thing which concerns us here is the art of letting go, freeing the heart and mind. In each letting go, the door of the heart opens for a single moment on infinity.

9
WHERE IS YOUR FAITH?

The reproach eases progressively from "How is it that you have no faith?" (Mark) to "Why are you fearful, O you of little faith?" (Matthew) to "Where is your faith?" (Luke). In Luke's story the implication is that the disciples do have faith but have, as it were, mislaid it. At the critical moment they are either unable to access it or forget to invoke it.

It is a thought-provoking question: **Where is your faith?** Where does it go when you are not using it? Is it humanly possible to keep your finger on it at all times? Or do we have only moments of faith, each one a gift of God? Is there such a thing as an abiding faith? If so, how do we learn to abide in it?

Since faith is, according to our teaching, the gift of God, not a natural human endowment, not something we can take for granted as part of our basic equipment, it seems that if it is to persist at all, there is greater likelihood of our being able to abide IN it than to keep our finger ON it; that is, to have it at our beck and call. Entering into the abode of faith is like entering the kingdom of Heaven, with the same entrance requirements.

Reflection: How would the story have unfolded had the disciples had faith?

10
A GREAT CALM.

"And he arose, and rebuked the wind, and said unto the sea, **'Peace, be still.'** And the wind ceased and there was a great calm" (Mk. 4:39). If Jesus had addressed himself to people with the same result, would we marvel? Yes, depending on the violence of the disturbance and suddenness of the calm. But when it is a question of affecting the brute forces of nature, and that with a single word, such as "Desist" or "Peace," we are confounded. Why the amazement? What can he do which we cannot?

We are capable of presence, we can communicate, we can have an effect on other people and on things. Even so, we can scarcely imagine what it is that he does which makes such an instant and total difference. Instead, suppose we imagine ourselves into the war of winds and the turmoil of the sea.

PEACE Meditation

Close your eyes and find a place in your body where you are **insisting**. Feel the LORD's hand touch that spot. Hear his voice say, **Peace!** Stay with that experience as long as you can. Then find a place in your body where you are **resisting**. Feel his hand touch that spot. Hear his voice say, **Peace!** Again, stay with the experience (feeling his touch, hearing his voice).

Now locate where in your body you may feel any degree of emotional distress, particularly a distress which follows from **insisting and resisting.** How does the distress express itself in your body? The sea expresses itself in waves. It heaves, boils, slams back and forth, floods, swamps and drowns, swallows and regurgitates. What is your emotion doing to you? Let the sound waves of the LORD's voice meet the waves of emotion with **Peace, be still.**

Enter into the great calm of the LORD's Presence, knowing that if you are out of control, He is nevertheless in control. "Say but the word and my soul shall be healed."

11
Vision IV
WHO IS THIS, THAT EVEN THE WIND AND THE SEA OBEY HIM?

Above — a strife of winds, below — a turmoil of waves. Conflicting perspectives warring in our brains, conflicting desires boiling in our guts. A single word, **Peace**, drops into the tumult and a change occurs, like waking from a bad dream. Everything clarifies, above and below, and falls into proper place. It is this we want to move through with strokes of color, the violent rending of the storm, the sudden and great calm, the question which runs through the whole like a penetrating breath, WHO?

The more you can get in touch with your own inner conflicts while making the picture, the truer the vision and the more useful for contemplation. How does a conflict of perspectives feel in your head? What kind of movement does it make? Describe that movement with your whole body. Let your body tell the story in its own way.

How does a conflict of desires feel in your belly? What does it do to your body? Allow your body to speak.

Now hear the LORD's voice uttering a great word, **Peace!** Feel the change in your belly; feel the change in your head. Afterwards, let your hands remember the storm, the calm, the **Who?** with color. The vividness of the experience will guide your hand, as will the miraculous experience of peace and clarity. WHO? is a breath of adoration and thanksgiving.

CONTEMPLATION

One thing guides the making of a picture, but another thing emerges. Sit face to face with that new thing and let it speak to you in its own way. From it you may learn a new mother tongue. It will relate a story previously unheard. It is the Good News.

12
WHO IS THIS?

"Who is this, that even the wind and the sea obey him?"

What did the disciples hope for from Jesus when they woke him, begging "Save us!"? Probably to have him pray for help, believing his prayers to be more efficacious than their own. He did not pray; he acted in the very manner one might hope for from the Creator of the universe. With a single word he touched the nerve centers of nature and the effect was instant.

Witnessing the miracle they feared a great fear. It is not like the panic which gripped them during the storm. It is a "great fear," one which lays open the mind to that which is beyond comprehension, one capable of blasting away the mind were it not for the efficacy of the one word, **Peace.** While their reaction to fear of the storm was off the mark (in the grip of that fear the mind was still capable of its misinterpretations), the spontaneous question which forms on their lips in the white light of the miracle is the most far-reaching one. Not **what** or **how**, or even **why**, but WHO. Calming the storm is not a technical feat but a miracle of Presence.

Once again feel the LORD's touch releasing you from where you **insist**, from where you **resist**, and silently (without using throat muscles) intone WHO.

WHO is a form of ultrasound. This we know since it is the one word attributed to the owl, the bird of wisdom. When Moses begs for the Name of the one who sends him to liberate Israel from Egypt, the response given is I AM WHO I AM (Ex. 3:14). Jesus puts the question to his disciples: WHO do people say I am?...WHO do you say I am? (Mt. 16:13, 15). The question WHO is the ultimate Christian koan, a riddle which functions as a mind/heart opener, a guide through the secret pass.

13
Vision V
THE FACE OF SUFFERING.

Reread the section of Mark's story on page 15 which describes the plight of the demoniac (5: 1-5). Then close your eyes and allow the image of the sufferer to take shape before your inner eye. See him as the LORD sees him. Consider his loneliness, his abandonment, his inability to master the forces which are tearing him apart, his shame, the nightmare of voices plaguing him within, his feeble attempts to destroy himself, his helpless desire to live. Let these considerations choose your colors and guide the movement of your hands. Through it all feel the LORD's compassion shining through.

CONTEMPLATION
Once the picture is finished put it aside for a few days. Wait until you can come back to it as a detached but sympathetic observer. Then begin to write down in words just what you see.

14
RECOGNITION I

"But when he saw Jesus afar off, he ran and fell at his feet..." (Mk. 5: 7)

In the story of the demoniac different modes and levels of recognition must be distinguished. Humanly speaking, the most effective mode and highest level of recognition is that of the sufferer himself. In the key story the disciples had no comprehension, from start to finish, of the meaning of Jesus' sleeping through the storm. They did not perceive him as the Eye of the storm, a center of stillness, of peace. By contrast, the demoniac recognizes immediately, the moment Jesus steps out of the boat, what he has sought vainly within himself, some place of peace, an area which the violence of the demons cannot touch or disturb.

The recognition of the demoniac is not in what he says (even though the pronoun 'I' is used), for the demons have taken over his voice. It is in his running to Jesus and throwing himself at his feet, which runs directly counter to the demons' challenge: "What have I to do with you?" The voice repels but the body beseeches.

The intensity and overwhelming character of his suffering, his desperate need prepared the demoniac for a recognition which escapes the disciples despite their privileged companionship. It is suffering which purifies the soul; it can be our most effective teacher.

REMEMBERING Meditation

Recall a particular instance of suffering in your life which prepared you for a recognition which might have eluded you otherwise. It may not be so terrible and hopeless a suffering as demonic possession. It must, however, be significant enough to have produced a turning-point in your life. It could be the death of someone dear to you; it could be an accident which has changed the course of your life; it could be the break-up of a relationship, financial loss or career failure; it could be a bad choice on your part which has set you on a different life-path. It could even be the normal circumstances of sickness, aging, and the prospect of death, which were the occasion of the Buddha's enlightenment and which he summed up in the first of the Four Noble Truths: "Existence is pain."

In a paragraph describe the precise form of the suffering and the circumstances of the recognition. Draw an arrow from the one to the other, pointing both ways. If a, then b; if b, then a. While the special form of your suffering may not be necessary for everyone (some may have reached a similar recognition without undergoing a like suffering), it is doubtful whether anyone can see the Face without entering into some aspect of the Passion of Christ. What you contemplate here is one step on your true path, one phase of your own soul-making.

15
THE TOMB DWELLER

The description of the demoniac, particularly vivid in Mark's story, provides clues to the exact nature of his sufferings. He is an extreme case, and thus a singularity, but he is at the same time an exemplar of a world without God, and thus universal. His sufferings are not foreign to what in us resists God. They are not foreign to whatever is guided exclusively by the spirit of the times, the **Zeitgeist,** our times every bit as much as those of the demoniac. Yet, in his extremity, the demoniac has become unfit for human community, unable to participate, unable to benefit, rejecting and rejected. He is a social outcast, a disturbance at every level and a reminder of what we do not wish to see. The only place he can find shelter is in the burial caves, among the dead.

But the tomb dweller is also a universal. At a psychological level he can represent either someone who is trapped in the past (the dead being the ghosts of the past), or someone who finds companionship only with finished men through the works they have left behind, who is either unable to cope with the give-and-take of the present or who is dissatisfied at heart by the apparent inconsequentiality of the day-to-day.

Jesus' answer to one of his disciples could as well have been directed to the tomb dweller, whether haunted or sustained by the attenuated presence of the dead: **Follow me; and let the dead bury their dead** (Mt. 8:22).

In Matthew's Gospel, just after Jesus says, "Let us pass over to the other side," there is a brief digression on the conditions for following Jesus. A scribe approaches and declares, "Master, I will follow you wherever you go." Jesus counters with, "Foxes have their lairs, and the birds of the air have nests; the Son of Man has nowhere to lay his head." A disciple says, "First let me bury my father," and Jesus counters, "Follow me; and let the dead bury their dead" (Mt. 8: 18-22).

In the precise context in which he places the sayings, Matthew probably has in mind letting go of the Jewish past, but the sayings themselves carry larger meanings which pertain to us and to our circumstances just as well as they did to the earliest Christian community. The saying, "...let the dead bury their dead," implies that those who are occupied with dead things are deadened by them. It includes all of those who are preoccupied by this world and its passing fashions, what's "in" and what's "out." The philosopher Hegel, analyzing the course of progress in history, claimed that consciousness progresses by way of negation. By burying those who have gone before (the past is passé), there comes a slight sense of being alive by contrast. But Hegel also called it "the path of doubt" and "a highway of despair." There is here no real movement from death to life; it is only the dead burying their dead.

To such questionable progress Jesus opposes an invitation, **Follow me,** but warns the enthusiast that the departure is radical, from nothing (the dead) to nowhere. He calls the demoniac out of the tombs to a wandering life, where he will be in this world but hardly of it, a parable and a paradox, a sign of contradiction, that the thoughts of many hearts may be revealed.

FOLLOWING Experiment

The Following of Christ is such a rich and venerable tradition in Christian practice that we can easily make the mistake of thinking that by consulting the tradition we can know just what it involves. It is true that a meditative study of biblical tradition and the lives of the saints opens to us heights and depths we might never have guessed otherwise. Even so, there is always a gap between then and now, there and here, them and me. Each destiny is unique and fashions the who we are in response to the who he is. John's path was not Peter's. "Peter, turning around, saw the disciple whom Jesus loved following them, the one who leaned on his breast at supper and said, "LORD, which is he that betrayeth thee?" Peter, seeing him, said to Jesus, "LORD, what about this man?" Jesus said to him, "If I have him stay behind till I come, what is that to you? Follow me." (Jn. 21: 20-22). Even following Jesus of Nazareth is not exactly the same as following the living Jesus.

There is a good reason why Jesus is no longer present among us in his singular human incarnation. While the human life of Jesus of Nazareth is for us an indispensable lens through which we learn how to see the world, ourselves, others, God, what we are looking at in our attempt to follow the living Jesus is

63

the course of our own lives with all that comes to bear upon that lifepath.

The two sayings encompassed within our story are clues to the following of the living Jesus, but they are both enigmatic. They tell us that true following has to do with moving from somewhere to nowhere and from death to life. But these instructions are very like the *neti...neti* of the Upanishads. Not this, not that...not here, not there.

Often clues turn up in unexpected places. Here is one from the ancient Chinese oracle, the I Ching, where it speaks of Earth in relation to Heaven. "Taking the lead, one goes astray; following, one finds the Master."[1] The usual procedure is reversed. Instead of knowing the Master (interpreted as Jesus of Nazareth), then following, it is a matter of first following, and through the experience of following, discovering the Master, the living Jesus.

But following what? Suppose we were to pay very close attention to the course of our own lives, even to the course of a single day, today, **watching for signs** (cf. the Gospel admonition to WATCH). Suppose we were to say to ourselves, Everything which belongs to my life (today) will enter it, everything which enters my life (today) belongs to it.[2] The saying stretches over the whole of my life, but actual following can only take place today, in the now moment. Following is actually a way of **becoming present to the Presence** in the here and now. Today is full of surprises for those with eyes to see. Following is to be **on the alert for surprises**, and to welcome them as belonging, as revelation of who and WHO. WHO is knocking at my door?

Welcoming whatever comes into my life as belonging to it does not determine how I shall relate to each and every thing. Some things I may well say "no" to, but I will say "yes" to the necessity of relating to them. Believing that whatever belongs to my life will come into it does not eliminate searching and seeking, but it suffuses the quest with a sense of peace. If it is meant for me, then I shall find it somewhere on my path. If I do not find what I seek, then I ask myself if I am failing to recognize what I do find offered to me.

Being on the alert for surprises is a way of cultivating spontaneity, of dancing on light feet down the road of life instead of plodding along doggedly. The living Jesus is the **spons** (the root) of spontaneity: the source, the fountain, the freely flowing, the drink-offering, the outpouring, the promise, the guarantor, the correspondent, the spouse of the soul.

Practice approaching "today" as an adventure into the unknown. Be on the alert for surprises, which may intrude upsetting your plans, or which may present themselves as mere hints, too easily ignored. Carry your body in such a way that you can turn at a moment's notice without losing your balance. Learn how to read events as signs by looking for the Presence in the present.

---

1 Thomas Cleary. *The Taoist I Ching* (Boston, 1966), p. 43.
2 I owe this guideline to my brother, John Dunne, *The Way of All the Earth* (New York, 1972), p. 203.

16
THE UNEXPLODED BOMB

Matthew describes the possessed as "exceeding fierce, so that no man might pass by that way" (8:28). Mark tells how the populace tried vainly to control the demoniac, some by efforts at taming him, some by fetters and chains which he smashed (5:4). In the tombs he howled like a maddened beast, cutting himself with stones in a pathetic effort to get the demon out. It brings to mind the experience of a modern woman, Mary Barnes, who describes her journey through madness. She writes:

"I was very frightened of this big bomb in me, all my anger. It was sapping my life away. Everything seemed to go into this terrible thing inside me. I couldn't spew it out...There was the urge to throw it out, to explode it, outside myself. As if trying to tear it out would get rid of it...It's a terrible experience, the shattering of the bomb, and the more you try to throw it out, by violence, the more it seems to cling, to stick inside you."*

The unexploded bomb is very like the storm in which the boat bearing Jesus and the disciples was caught crossing the sea of Galilee, except that they were caught inside the storm whereas for the demoniac the storm is caught inside him. Imagine the demoniac, inside him the storm, inside the storm the boat and the panicky disciples, in the back of the boat the LORD, sleeping.

*M. Barnes and J. Berke. *Mary Barnes: Two Accounts of a Journey through Madness* (New York, 1972), p. 179.

IT Meditation

Mary Barnes referred to the unexploded bomb inside herself as IT. Find where IT is located inside your body. Place your hand over that spot in your body. How does IT feel to you? Can you feel how IT sucks up your life force? What does IT do inside you? How would you get rid of IT if you could? Is there any way to be rid of IT without harming yourself or someone else?

Now feel IT as a storm going on inside you. Find in that maelstrom a tiny boat. Hear the frightened shouts of the disciples. Reach past the panic to a sleeping Presence. Now what do you do?

17
RECOGNITION II

Usurping the voice of the sufferer, IT cries out: "What have I to do with you, Jesus, Son of the Most High God? I adjure you by God, torment me not" (Mk. 5:7). In today's street speech IT is saying, "Back off! This is my turf and my time!" (in Matthew's story the demons add: "Have you come here to torment us before the time?" [8:29]). The moment that Jesus steps out of the boat and onto pagan territory signals a new era where all the rules change. It is to this that the demons loudly object.

Thus far the action. At the knowledge level what strikes us as amazing is the instant and precise recognition of WHO it is who has invaded their space/time. They are not put off by the humble human form. They are not confused and slow to learn, as are the disciples. They know exactly and with certainty. **How do they know?** Perhaps by a sense of the power which overmasters their own, for they cannot refuse his command, "Come out of the man, unclean spirit!"

If the **how** of their knowledge is amazing, there is nevertheless a much more disturbing question to be asked about their knowledge.

Reflection: Why does it do them no good?

We often think that if we knew for certain that Jesus is who the Gospels say he is, then we would not hesitate to become true followers. What prevents us are the doubts, the uncertainties, and the whole critical apparatus of the modern age which makes it all seem so unlikely, so naive. Yet here is an example of superior knowledge which makes no difference at all to the life. "And there was in their synagogue a man with an unclean spirit; and he cried out, saying, 'Let us alone; what have we to do with you, Jesus of Nazareth? Have you come to destroy us? I know who you are, the Holy One of God.' " (MK. 1:23-24). It does not save; it does not transform. Their recognition of Jesus is like the recognition of light by those who hate it "And this is the condemnation, that light has come into the world, and men loved darkness rather than light, because their deeds were evil. For everyone who does evil hates the light, and does not come to the light, lest his deeds should be reproved" (Jn. 3: 19-20).

18
WHAT IS YOUR NAME? A

The only person in the story (key story as well as frame story) who has a real name is **Jesus = Yeshuah = Yahweh saves.** His name names him; it gives away his secret. "Gives away" is used here deliberately, since to know the name is to have a fix on someone. But, to whom is his name a real giveaway? Only to those who can understand the true meaning of **Yahweh saves.** Those who can understand it are the beneficiaries of that salvation (for others the words are empty), which rules out "using." For instance, in the story the demoniac is the only person who really knows the name. Even the disciples are excluded. They can at best raise the question, "WHO?" It is an irony of the story that while the disciples are of course well aware that their master calls himself Jesus, and while the knowledge of the demons is as precise as one could ask, it is only the demoniac who cannot speak, but in the total gesture casts himself at Jesus' feet, who knows.

In Jewish lore many of the demons do have names, but when Jesus demands the name, the answer is "legion, for we are many." A collective name rather than a proper name; a collective which points to the oppressive presence of the Roman occupation. (A Roman legion was composed of between 4000 and 6000 men). Here the name serves both as a pun and a clue. As is the Roman presence to the entire population, so the demonic presence to the sufferer; a massive IT made up of a nameless multitude. To get an idea of what the suffering is like, we might think, on the one hand, of some of the characteristics of a nameless mob and, on the other hand, of what it would be like to be part of an army of occupation and what it would be like to live under the heel of a foreign army.

To understand the sufferer in his demoniacal condition we must experience both roles, oppressor and oppressed. The story divides the roles by personifying the demons, while leaving them nameless, but we need to remember that the human individual and the demonic multitude are tangled together in one body.

Mob psychology is a kind of infection, an intoxication. One is caught up in the mood of the moment, borne along by the strength of the many, exalted, irresistible. The movement of the mob is like an avalanche, sweeping everything along in its inexorable path. Thinking is submerged, responsibility vanishes, and with these go caring and compassion. All that we associate with "humanity" is gone, in an instant, as though it had never been. No wonder the ancients called it 'demonic,' witnessing such power, so inimical to the hard-won gains of human consciousness. If we were to compare the emergence of human spirit (true humanity) to the slow growth of a tree, the contagion of mob psychology would be like a raging forest fire. It was the mob that murdered Jesus.

By contrast, to have a name would be to take responsibility, to refuse the easy way out and the security of numbers. "I said it, I did it, I, so-and-so, am the one you seek." To give the name as legion is to cop out, to hide behind the anonymity of the mob. "Everybody is doing it, everybody thinks this way, why blame me? Can so many people be wrong?"

Armies of occupation are notoriously amoral. It is interesting how being transplanted geographically for a short period of time, where no one knows you, where you do not have your life, can as it were erase all the memory banks. Conduct which might never have been considered "at home" is suddenly greeted by, "Why not?" "No one (who counts) will ever know." And does the individual himself or herself not know? Does God not know?

A sudden and total abandonment of moral and religious culture is a frightening phenomenon to witness in others and to experience in oneself. Are the values we cherish nothing but a veneer? Is demonic laughter waiting for us in the wings once we have strutted our hour upon the stage?

There is in the face of so much violence and so much oblivion a temptation to despair of the possibility of spirit. And yet the real delusion may not be in the direction of spirit but in the direction of the mass and massiveness. What happens to the "many" in "Many are called, but few are chosen"? Recently, chaos theory has pointed out what it calls the Butterfly Effect, how a butterfly stirring the air in one part of the world today can transform storm systems on the opposite side of the world next month. In like manner, an individual who opts for spirit over against the weight of the mob, even if, like the demoniac, all he can do is cast himself mutely at the feet of his savior, or like Jesus, lay down his life willingly at the feet of his God, may have an incalculable effect on humanity as a whole.

BUTTERFLY Visualization

How do you earn the right to say 'I'? How do you separate yourself from the mob? How do you hold on to mind and heart when it would be so easy to slide into violence and oblivion? Think of your feeble efforts towards true humanity as the delicate flutter of a butterfly's wings. Remember how often you think, "I'm not getting anywhere with this. What good does it do?" Now imagine the tiny stir your fluttering has made. The tiny stir makes a subtle, imperceptible difference in wind currents. The weather pattern diverges ever so slightly, then a bit more. Before long the shift is perceptible, then significant. It reaches a tempest blowing over the sea of Galilee and divides the battling winds. It reaches a storm raging in the body of one poor sufferer on the other side of the lake and is like a cool breeze bringing him relief.

I-AM-I Mantra. Close your eyes. Hear your own voice re-sounding in your head, saying "I am I, not 'them,' not 'us,' " Hear it vibrating in your throat, in your breast, your belly, your hands, your feet.

19
WHAT IS YOUR NAME? B

There is a Zen story about a wrestler named O-nami, (Great Waves) who was so bashful that when he performed in public he lost all his enormous strength. He went to a Zen master for help. The master told him, "Great Waves is your name. Stay in the temple tonight and imagine that you are huge waves sweeping and swallowing everything in your path." The master returned in the morning and found O-nami meditating, a faint smile on his face. The master touched him. "Go now," he said, "nothing can disturb you; nothing can resist you." O-nami was never again defeated in public.[1]

Our problem is that we do not have essence names. Philosophers would explain that it is because our essence (our "who" more so than our "what") is either unknown or unknowable, because unfinished. So long as life goes on we are still in the making. Who we are will only come clear at the end, if ever. Even when a life is finished, there may be multiple interpretations of that life. It remains a mystery from without, from the point of view of the observer. It is also a mystery from within, from the point of view of the living subject. Which of us knows **who** we really are?

We know of One who has a true name, One who is neither finished (in the sense of ended, over) nor unfinished (still in the making), One alone who can say, I AM WHO I AM, or just I AM. In the Lord's Prayer we are told by our Master to hallow the Name. How is it done?

Muslim tradition teaches that there are 300 names of God in the Torah, 300 names in the Psalms, 300 names in the New Testament, 99 in the Qur'an, and one hidden Name. Muslims have a spiritual practice called *dhikrullah* (remembering God) wherein the practitioner either chooses or receives from a shaikh, a spiritual guide, one of the 99 Qur'anic names. The chosen name is repeated day and night in such a way that the supplicant enters into the name and participates to some degree in the Being of God, much as O-nami entered into his own name and became Great Waves.

"Not unto us, O LORD, not unto us, but unto thy name give glory, for thy mercy and for thy truth's sake" (Psalm 115). It is not a matter of stealing for oneself that which belongs only to God, but of relinquishing self into the Being of God. A Muslim story relates how a certain poor shaikh would pray *la ilaha* (there is no god) and disappear, and *illa'llah* (but God) and reappear.[2] It is a paradox. This nameless self disappears into the Being of God; who is it who reappears?

HALLOWING THE NAME Meditation

Even though we don't know our own name, by the grace of revelation we do know the name(s) of our God. An affinity which we may feel for one name more than another may well be a hint in the direction of our own proper name. Tradition teaches that repetition of a divine name conforms us in some degree to that facet of the Being of God. The danger of the practice is one of psychic inflation, the possibility of confusing ourselves with an aspect of God, effectively substituting god for God. A way to have the transfiguring good of the practice while avoiding its built-in danger is to emulate the poor shaikh's habit of appearing and disappearing. This we can do according to a model found in the fourth book of the collection, *Zen Flesh, Zen Bones*, which Paul Reps calls "Centering" and which is itself a compilation of 112 modes of meditation. Shiva presents the 112 modes in response to a question posed by his beloved, Devi. Here are the first four modes:

1. Radiant one, this experience may dawn between two breaths. After breath comes in (down) and just before turning up (out) — **the beneficence.**
2. As breath turns from down to up, and again as breath curves from up to down — through both these turns, **realize.**
3. Or, whenever inbreath and outbreath fuse, at this instant touch the energyless energy-filled **center.**
4. Or, when breath is all out (up) and stopped of itself, or all in (down) and stopped — in such universal pause, one's small self vanishes. This is difficult only for the impure.

Here is my suggestion, modelled on John 17: 21. On the inbreath pray "Thou in me," on the outbreath "and I in Thee." Between the breaths silently speak the chosen Name in your heart. With "Thou in me" appear, with "and I in Thee" disappear.

---

1 see Paul Reps. *Zen Flesh, Zen Bones* (New York, 1959), pp. 25-26.
2 Shems Friedlander. *Ninety-Nine Names of ALLAH* (New York, 1978), pp. 16-18.

20
WHAT IS YOUR NAME? C

Besides the 999 names in Torah, Psalms, New Testament and Qur'an, there is the hidden Name. There is also our own true name, unknown and unknowable, humanly speaking. But our LORD says that "there is nothing covered, that shall not be revealed; and hid, that shall not be known" (Mt. 10:26). To those who overcome he promises the hidden manna and a white stone, "and in a stone a new name written, which no one knows save the one who receives it" (Rv. 2:17). Those who overcome will be made pillars in the temple of God, and upon them will be written "the name of my God, and the name of the city of my God, new Jerusalem, which cometh down out of heaven from my God: and my new name" (Rv. 3:12).

Those who overcome are the ones who succumb neither to the temptation to slip back into the anonymity and irresponsibility of the mob nor to that of scrambling forward into the paradisal sin of taking for themselves what belongs only to God. The book of Revelation implies a connection between one's own true name and the hidden Name of God. There may also be a connection between overcoming the twin but opposite temptations and learning the hidden names of self and God.

The connector is the experience of being called by God and of responding to that call.

How is the divine call experienced? For the most part through the deep longing of the heart. Early in life it is no mean task to identify that longing, and to sort out the divine Voice from a multitude of other voices prompting on every side. To follow the deep longing requires purification of the heart and true guidance.

Later on, when the divine Voice falls silent, the heart darkens. The soul drops its wings. The proper course is to fast and wait, to learn obedience in humility. Enthusiasm, which means literally to be filled with God, is gone, and the soul becomes more vulnerable than before to the beckonings of lesser voices. If these voices are followed and one strays from the narrow path, then vulnerability becomes actual wounding. From a darkening of the light to a wounding of the bright.*

Afterwards, the divine Voice is heard once again, but the sound of the Voice is no longer delight but pure pain. There may be a wish to hide from it, the way Adam and Eve tried to hide after their sin when the LORD God called, "Where are you?" (Gn. 3:9). But the only hope is for the soul to embrace the pain and the guilt, and for the heart to break open. If true repentance occurs, the wounding is transfigured, conjoined to the mystery of the sacred wounds of Christ, and the broken heart is enabled

---

*These images are drawn to some extent from hexagram 36 of the *I Ching*, where darkening is imaged by light buried under earth (cf. humus, humility) and wounding is imaged by the firebird of the soul (bright pheasant) brought down by an arrow.

to participate in the outpouring of water, blood and Spirit by which the world is saved.

But one of the soldiers with a spear pierced his side, and forthwith came there out blood and water (Jn. 19: 34).

This is he that came by water and blood, Jesus Christ; not by water only, but by water and blood. And it is the Spirit that bears witness, because the Spirit is truth. For there are three that bear record, the Spirit, and the water, and the blood: and these three agree in one (I Jn. 5: 6-8).

If life were straightforward, if sin were not a factor, would our true name still be hidden? I think so. We believe we are living (or are meant to live) one story when in truth we are living a different and lesser (since we invariably fail to realize our ideal self), yet far greater story. Even Jesus thought he had been sent only for the lost sheep of the house of Israel, a task at which he failed

(O Jerusalem, Jerusalem, which kills the prophets, and stones them that are sent to you; how often would I have gathered your children together, as a hen gathers her brood under her wings, but you would not! Lk. 13: 34)

when in fact, and through that very failure, he is sent for all mankind.

For He has said:

"It is not enough that you be for me a servant to raise up the tribes of Jacob and bring back the survivors of Israel: I have destined you to be the light of the nations, that My salvation may reach the ends of the earth (Is. 49: 6).

I say then, Have they stumbled that they should fall? God forbid: but rather through their fall salvation is come unto the Gentiles, to provoke them to jealousy (Rm. 11: 11).

Mary thought her task was to be the mother of Jesus of Nazareth, and it is through her failures that she learns to become mother of God.

And when they saw him, they were amazed: and his mother said to him, Son, why have you treated us this way? Your father and I have sought you sorrowing. And he said to them, Why did you seek me? Do you not know that I must be about my Father's business? (Lk. 2: 48-49).

...the mother of Jesus said to him, They have no wine. Jesus answered her, Woman, what have I to do with you? My hour has not yet come. His mother told the servants, Whatever he tells you, do it. (Jn. 2: 3-5).

Jesus came into the house, and once again the crowd gathered, to such a point that they could not even take their meal. And when his family heard of it, they went to take hold of him, saying, He is out of his head (Mk. 3: 20-21).

There are divine reasons why our true story (hence, our true name) is unknown to us. For one thing we have no way of measuring the consequences of our actions, how the humble, everyday things we are doing and suffering could possibly have such a grand repercussions. For another, it is far better for the health of our soul in this life not to see. The only things we do which are genuinely pure of heart are those done unknowingly. To be self-regarding in doing good is to have one's reward. Then, the value of the action does not transcend the momentary satisfaction.

Even an erring life, a more complicated story, can prove in the long run to be a greater story. Blessed Julian of Norwich proclaims, "Sin is behovely." It behooves and, in the long run, it is lovely, if through its turnings the heart of God is better revealed.

TEN DONKEYS

In the 12th century a Chinese master, named Kakuan, drew Ten Bulls to illustrate through pictures and verse the steps leading to enlightenment.* He chose the bull as representing the life-principle going through a sequence of ten transformations. Recall in your own life an incident of going astray (making an ass of yourself). In a series of cartoons, whether ten or however many, draw the sequence of events — how you were lost and how you were found — with an appropriate verse relating the deeper meaning of each cartoon.

83

You may also, if you wish, add a prose comment, as did Kakuan. Let it become a divine comedy. A donkey seems appropriate to a Christian sequence, not only for its comic associations but because the LORD honored the humble beast by choosing it as the vehicle which carried him to his Passion and Resurrection.

*A version of the Ten Bulls can be found in Paul Reps. *Zen Flesh, Zen Bones.*

21
A SEA CHANGE

Modern sensibilities balk at the prospect of sending the demons into a nearby herd of pigs. The victimization of innocent animals may be so offensive to our newfound awareness of animal rights that it can prevent an understanding of the story from this point on. In order to continue we have to make an effort to think our way into another mentality. From the then current Jewish point of view swine were unclean animals, that is, unfit for human consumption. Jesus also refers to the demon(s) as "unclean." Just as holy things are reserved for the holy, so an unclean spirit belongs in an unclean residence. More to the point are the metaphorical associations. Jewish feeling at the time made a kind of equation between the Romans and swine, particularly because the pig has a cloven hoof and so appears to be a "clean" animal, but does not chew the cud, so is in fact unclean. Just so, Roman law appears to typify a developed sense of justice, but the Roman presence was in fact demoralizing and corrupt. If the demoniac in his possessed state manifests the spiritual condition of society at large, there is a felt appropriateness in banishing the offense back to the metaphorical domain of the offender. The Legion should be "at home" in the swine.

In a more general sense, it is important to place the demons somewhere rather than letting them roam about at large, whereabouts unknown. It may also have been a particularly happy thought, as it turned out, to send them into a herd of animals, creatures of instinct. It was a healthy instinct which drove the pigs into the sea.

The pigs drown in the sea and the demons drown with them. They undergo a sea change, dissolving and resolving. We may think of it as a pig sacrifice which allows evil configurations to be broken up under the influence of sea water, to be resolved into atoms, and there in the great maternal womb to be recombined and eventually born anew to a new chance and fresh possibilities. It is a kind of baptism, a far happier outcome than if the demons had simply been held in some sterile place in perpetual confinement.

TO SOLVE, DISSOLVE

Sometimes readjustment is not enough; what is needed is radical change, a kind of unmaking and remaking. What are the signs? When you can no longer go on as before, having no energy for it, and fall prostrate, seeing no clear path either ahead or behind, it is time for the old life to dissolve. Imagine yourself dissolving literally, first in tears, then in sweat, and finally in blood. There is kinship between blood, sweat, tears and seawater, the universal solvent, but there is also a translation from a purely physical to a physicospiritual level.

(1) **Dissolving in Tears.** What would you weep for? For what is past and gone? For what might have been? For what is not

to be? For who you are and who you are not? Jesus wept for Lazarus and for Jerusalem. It is okay to mourn. But there is another kind and another level of weeping. There are tears of joy, of release from bondage. Tears which are like rain watering the earth and rendering it fruitful. What would it take to move from one level of tears to another?

(2) **Dissolving in Sweat.** What makes you sweat? Exertion, anxiety, fear? Jesus suffered a bloody sweat in the garden of Gethsemane. It is okay to be afraid. But there is also the sweat that comes when the fever breaks. There is the sweat that rids the body of impurities. There is the sweat lodge, a place of purification and preparation. What would it take to move from one level of sweating to another?

(3) **Dissolving in Blood.** What makes you bleed? Hemorrhage, self-inflicted injury, whether accidental or intended, violence? Jesus suffered the violence of others. It is possible to survive violation and violence, spiritually if not physically. Jesus was able to transmute an act of violence into an oblation, completely,

My Father loves me because I lay down my life, that I might take it up again. No one takes it from me, but I lay it down of my own accord. (Jn. 10: 17-18).

What would it take to move from bloodshed to a sacramental outpouring?

22
Vision VI
The Face of Healing

What change comes over the demoniac once the demons are expelled? Will the people who knew him before recognize him still? The Gospel says only that he is "sitting, and clothed, and in his right mind." How do you see him?

1. Let the picture make itself spontaneously, choosing its own form and colors. Do not read the remainder of the instructions until you are satisfied that the picture is complete.

2. Write down in detail an account of how the picture came to be. What images or movements came to you first, what decided the colors, etc. Include your own reading of the picture, the significance of the shapes and colors, what is happening in the picture.

3. How do you know what the Face of Healing would be like? It is because healing has already occurred or is occurring in you? Where in the picture is the source of healing? What is being healed?

CONTEMPLATION

Place the two visions, the Face of Suffering and the Face of Healing side by side. Could it be the same face? How do they affect one another? What do they say to one another?

23
RECOGNITION III

The pigherders run with the news to city and countryside. The people come out to see. There is a superficial resemblance to the scene of the Samaritan woman running to her village with the news, "Come, see a man who told me all things that ever I did: is not this the Christ?" (Jn. 4:29), and their following her back to the well to see for themselves. The crucial difference is that both she and her fellow villagers saw and believed, while in the present scene the pigherders are intent on pointing the blame for the loss of the herd away from themselves, and the people who come out to see are afraid and ask Jesus to leave.

What did they see: They saw (probably in this order) that the pigs were gone, that the madman whom they could control neither by persuasion nor by force was "sitting, and clothed, and in his right mind," and that the one responsible was a certain Jew from across the lake, who was standing there with some other Galileans. What they saw made them afraid. What they saw when they saw Jesus was a threat. Meager as it is, it is a true seeing. They saw the sign of contradiction, which has come for the rise and fall of many, and not only in Israel (Lk. 2:34). Those who can rise by that sign are only those who can

91

first of all fall by it. It was that loss and fall which the Gadarenes refused.

Until that moment they could look upon the demoniac as an anomaly, a public nuisance, something less than human, unfit and harmful to their society. Now, even if it is not brought to full consciousness, there lurks in the back of their minds a recognition of a connection between the herd of pigs, their livelihood, and the suffering condition of the demoniac. These were people who perhaps profited from the Roman occupation, who accommodated themselves to Roman ways, who knew which way the wind was blowing, economically speaking. They are faced now with a most uncomfortable choice, health of soul or profit. They must see that the disturbing presence of the demoniac was a faithful mirror, reflecting not their success-ful outer selves but the misery of their souls. It is something they choose not to see. They ask Jesus, he who holds the mirror, to leave their country.

The marvel is not the refusal of the Gadarenes, but the Samaritans' willingness to recognize as the Christ one who shows them all things that they ever did. Even so, it is stunning to think about the opportunity which came their way, which they considered and contemplated...and refused.

Socrates once said that he had rather be refuted than refute, if only the truth might win (Gorgias 458a). How can we, like Socrates, learn to love truth better than self? How did the Samaritan woman get past the pain of self-revelation? She too experienced a discomfort not unlike that of the Gadarenes when the LORD reminded her of her chequered marital history. She tried to change the subject, bringing up the old debate about the proper place of worship, then dismissing it all with an offhand remark about "when the Messiah comes...". Jesus cuts right through the smokescreen with I AM (he). The next thing we know she has dropped her waterpot and run for her neighbors with the great news.

She too had been trying to protect her little self, just like the Gadarenes, but when confronted with the one WHO IS, she dropped that little self like a discarded waterpot, one too small to hold the gift of living water.

I AM Mantra

What magical thing happened between one moment when the Samaritan woman was dancing away from the sword of truth and the next when she simply forgot her old waterpot self? She heard the LORD's Voice saying, I AM.

Sit quietly and let the Voice resound through your body like a deep bell, I AM. (It is different from most mantric meditations in that it is the LORD's Voice you hear, not your own). No matter what...I AM. No matter how much you may have lied, cheated, stolen up to this moment...I AM. No matter what a mess you have made of your life...I AM. No matter how ugly the sight of your own soul...I AM. No matter how much time you have wasted...I AM. I AM here for you. I AM yours.

24
TO BE WITH THE LORD

The twelve were chosen first of all to "be with him," and then to preach, heal sicknesses and cast out devils (Mk. 3:14-15). Why is it that when the healed sufferer asks to "be with him," he is not allowed (Mk. 5:18-19)? When we consider that he had a better understanding of the LORD than did the chosen twelve, why is he not permitted to join the inner circle? We might even expect him to become the first of the apostles, the beloved disciple.

These questions may remind us of a certain debate carried on quietly by the twelve among themselves later on, concerning which of them was the greatest, or the request of the mother of the sons of Zebedee that her sons might sit at the LORD's right and left hand in his kingdom. To these concerns Jesus replies with a series of enigmas. He tells them, "whoever wishes to be first, let him become last of all and the servant of all" (Mk. 9:35). Then he shows them the mystery of the Child, to which we could attach all the sayings concerning spiritual childhood. Finally, he tells the sons of Zebedee that it is not for him (Jesus) to grant such a request, but "it shall be given to them for whom it is prepared" (Mk. 10:40).

You will object that the desire to be with the LORD is not the same as the desire to be first or to have the lion's share of power and glory. It is very true, but not immediately obvious due to the ambiguities of the image of being "next to" the LORD.

I think we can safely assume that the desire of the healed sufferer is pure of heart. He is not asking for glory. He is asking for privilege, for it is indeed a privilege to be with the LORD. It may strike us as unfair that bunglers were granted such a privilege, while one purified in the crucible of suffering was not. Perhaps we should keep in mind, however, that the nearness of the twelve to Jesus and their privileged witnessing was in view of a special task to be performed later on and, as is obvious from their reactions, is not to be equated with closeness in the truest spiritual sense. Physical proximity and spiritual communion are two very different things. If it were not so, we should all find ourselves at a serious disadvantage, removed as we are by two thousand years.

It may well be, in fact it must be the case that the healed sufferer did not really need what he so desired, whereas the twelve, still untried, did. The healed man is one who has already received into the cleansed hollow of his being the gift of living water, and who has become himself a source ("In the last day, that great day of the feast, Jesus stood and cried, saying, 'Let whoever thirsts come to me and drink. Whoever believes in me, as Scripture says, from his bosom shall flow rivers of living water' " (Jn. 7: 37-38)). While he may feel alone and impoverished, exiled in a world far from God, he has nevertheless the inestimable ability to touch the living source at any moment and to draw from it for the sake of others.

SPIRITUAL COMMUNION

"I will not leave you orphans; I will come to you" (Jn. 14:18). The healed sufferer has participated in advance in the Passion and Resurrection of the LORD. He knows already the risen Presence of the LORD, which has none of the limitations of physical presence. Ordinary presence, even in situations of greatest intimacy, suffers from difficulties of communication, of differing needs, and in general of "otherness." The Divine Presence, which the risen Presence incarnates most perfectly, while perceptible only to the purified soul, and even then paradoxically, surpasses infinitely one's presence even to oneself. The Qur'an expresses it poetically: "We indeed created man; and We know what his soul whispers within him, and We are nearer to him that the jugular vein" (50:16, Arberry tr.). Nearer to us than our very life, more intimately united to us than the union of soul and body, residing (according to Meister Eckhart) in the very core of our being, a core of which we ourselves are only remotely and indirectly aware, that Presence is the heaven of the saint and the hell of the sinner.

Suppose we return to the scene of the encounter between Jesus and the Samaritan woman, and to the interchange between them on the subject of living water (Jn. 4:7-15). **Imagine your own soul as a very deep well.** The LORD is sitting on the edge of the well, and says to you: "Give me to drink." It may well be that we can only draw water from our own well when we are willing to give it away.

You demur.   "Surely you don't want my water. Nobody
                      wants my water."

He replies: "If you knew the gift of God..."
                      "and who it is who asks..."

"you would have asked him..."

"and he would have given you living water."

Such is our ignorance. We have no idea WHO it is who resides at our well. We have no idea of the worth and virtue of what our well contains. We have no idea how to reach that water. The solution escapes us because it is so simple. What could be easier, and yet what could be more difficult and more demanding (our all), than to ask. **Dare to ask.**

25
BECOMING A PARABLE

Jesus says to the healed sufferer, **Go home to your own people, and tell them the great things the LORD has done for you, and how he has had compassion on you.** The most striking feature of the conclusion of the story is the continued mercy of the LORD towards a people which has refused him. The presence of the healed sufferer in their midst is a continuing opportunity to seize the amazing grace offered to them. The sufferer had always been a parable of sorts. His suffering condition had been a mirror of the frightful state of their souls. His healed condition is a parable of a higher order, mirroring the possibility which remains open to them. If at any time they decide to follow this parable, they too can become parables and with that be rid of all their daily cares.

It is what we ourselves have been attempting to do through these exercises, to follow the parable, to make it real not only to our minds but in our lives. Kafka's parable on parables continues:

"Another said: I bet that is also a parable."
"The first said: You have won."
"The second said: But unfortunately only in parable."

"The first said: No, in reality: in parable you have lost."

The interlocutor has followed the parable in mind, but not in life. He has failed to become a parable.

If we cannot become parables just by understanding them, neither can we do so by trying self-consciously to follow them in life. Imitating a parable is just that, an imitation, not the real thing. What does it take to become the real thing? "Go over." Better still, "Let us pass over unto the other side."

CONTEMPLATING THE LORD

Once I had a friend who asked me how to make an examination of conscience. She explained her difficulty. "I look at the LORD and I forget to look at myself." And so she arrives at the opposite shore, perhaps without remembering how she got there. Lost in the LORD, she is found. If we look long at what the LORD is doing, we need not worry about what we are doing. It is equivalent to St. Augustine's, "Love, and do what you will."

26
Vision VII
THE EYE OF THE STORM

We have reached the end of the story, an end which is also an unending beginning. We may now contemplate the story as a whole in the form of a *mandala*. A mandala is a mode of centering, well known to Eastern religions and to Navajo sand-painting ceremonials (where a sufferer sits in the middle of the painting and is thus restored to unity and harmony). It is also known to Christianity in the form of some of the great rose windows of our cathedrals. In a mandala we visualize all the elements, both hostile and friendly, involved in a given situation in terms of the center to which they relate, whether flowing to or from.

In Chapter 16, "The Unexploded Bomb," we visualize the whole momentarily. "Imagine the demoniac, inside him the storm, inside the storm the boat and the panicky disciples, in the back of the boat the LORD, sleeping." At that moment we were still experiencing it from the outside in, from the position of the trapped sufferer reaching towards what seemed to be an inaccessible Source of peace. Now we are ready to begin from that center of peace, the potent Eye of the storm, which holds together the whole, radiating outward. It is the paradox of a sleeping Eye, perhaps half-closed like the eye of a Buddha, one apparently unconcerned with the violence and suffering of the world, but one which holds together what would otherwise fly apart.

How do you see that sleeping Presence touching, connecting the disparate elements which surround it?

Mandalas usually take a geometric form, made up of concentrically related circles and squares, or radial and spherical arrangements. Keep in mind that your picture need not be representational. Color, movement, placement may be all you need. What you are looking for is **the feeling of the whole.** Let that feeling be your guide. You may not see the whole in advance or know exactly what you want to do. Begin at the center, working outward, and let it come together beneath your fingers.

CONTEMPLATION

In a story reality unfolds sequentially. In a mandala it comes back together in a single interrelated moment, like eternity. Gazing at the mandala, feel your own disparate parts, your suffering and your peace, coming together in your ownmost Center which owns you, all of you.

Personal Reflections and Recollections